Button Box

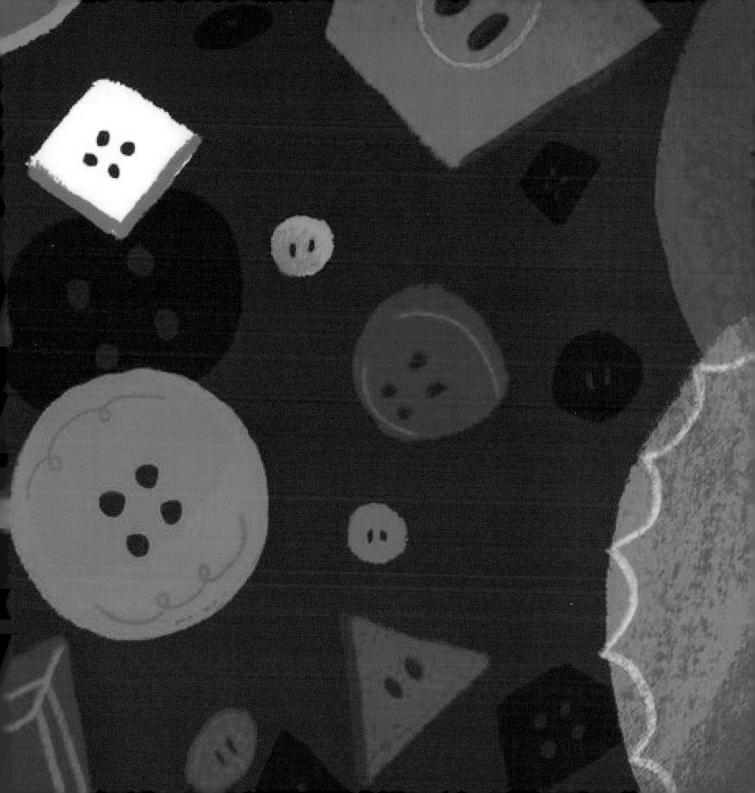

Red button

Blue button

Old button

New Button

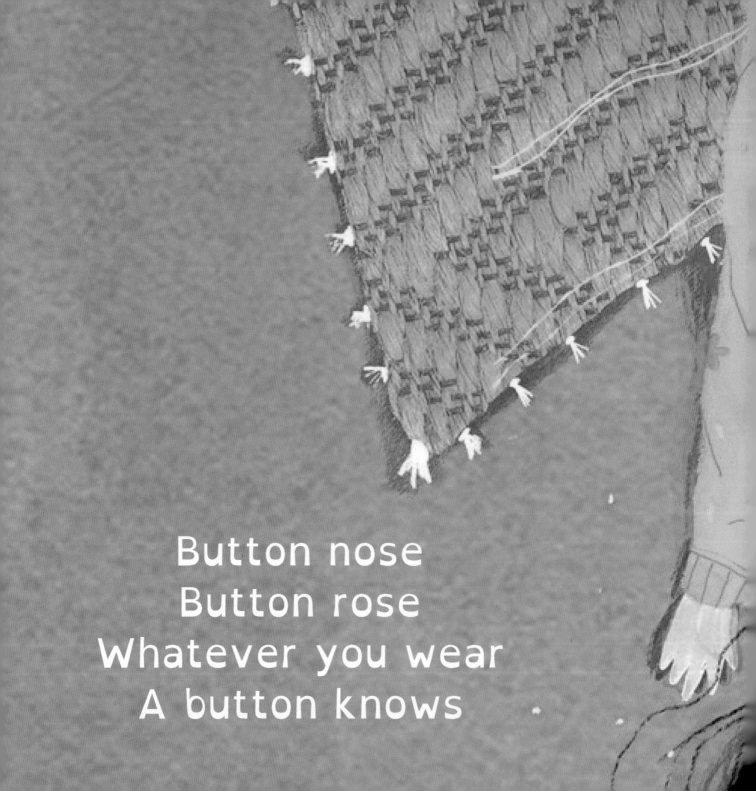

Button nose
Button rose
Whatever you wear
A button knows

Button box
Button bowl
If you
stumble
Buttons roll

Down the drain
Behind the drapes
This is how
A button escapes

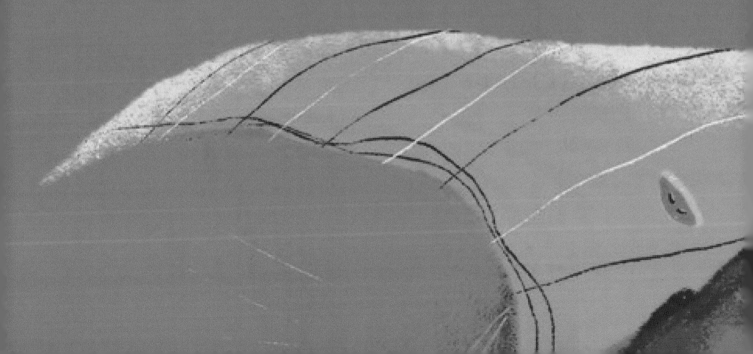

If they break
You can stitch them If
they're lost
Simply switch them

Twist and turn
Pull and clutch
With buttons you can
Expect too much

Better than a zip
Better than a
string Solid and
reliable Buttons
are your thing

They ask no questions They tell no lies

(Just stay away
From button
eyes.)

Button faded
Button shiny
Button
enormous
Button tiny

Button round
Button square
Button where?
Button there!

Bottom button
Button top
Button, button,
button

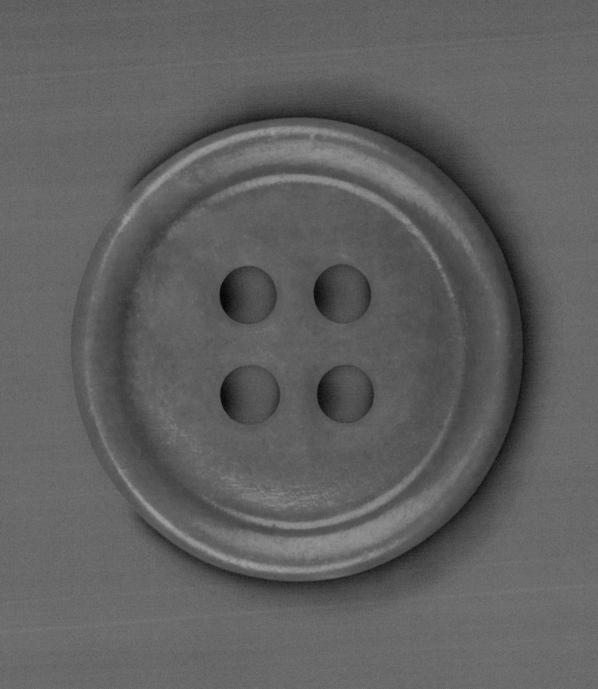

Printed in Great Britain
by Amazon

22359390R00016